Mashburn

W9-CJF-455

FOR LIZA

Copyright © 1991 by Cynthia Jabar

First Edition

Library of Congress Cataloging-in-Publication Data

Jabar, Cynthia.
    Bored blue? — think what you can do!—1st ed.
        p. cm.
    Summary. A young girl relates, in verse, all the things she loves
and would love to do, from "squishing-squashing in the mud" to
"swimming in a chocolate sea."
    ISBN 0-316-43458-2
    [1. Stories in rhyme.] I. Title.
PZ8.3.J124Bo   1991
[E]—dc20   90-33753

Joy Street Books are published by Little, Brown and Company (Inc.)

10 9 8 7 6 5 4 3 2 1

WOR
Published simultaneously in Canada by
Little, Brown and Company (Canada) Limited

Printed in the United States of America

BORED BLUE?
think what you can do!

CYNTHIA JABAR

Little, Brown and Company
Boston Toronto London

When I'm bored
and when I'm blue,
I name the things I love to do.
Can you?

I love squishing-squashing in the mud,

kicking balls that end up, THUD!

raking leaves,

and swinging high,

little earth and great big sky!

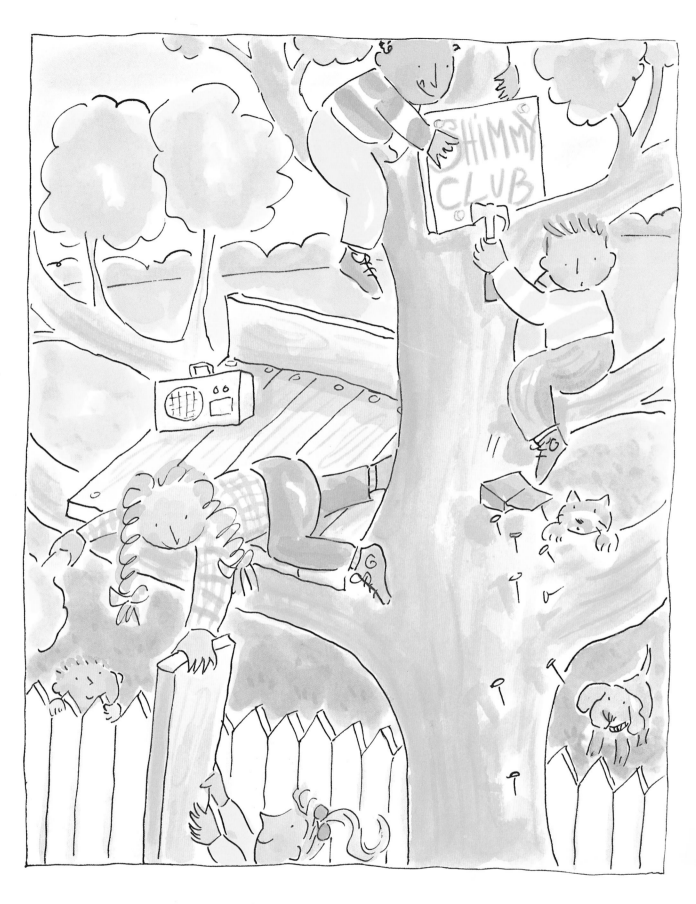

I love making cabins out of wood,

riding through my neighborhood,

mixing red and purple-pink,

skating on a skating rink.

I love cowboy hats,

and books galore,

go-go dancin' on the floor,

eating jam and buttered toast,

or scuba diving off the coast.

I'd love dining with the Queen of Crete,

tightrope walking without my feet,

surfing high on a sea of foam,

or traveling someplace far from home.

I'd love swimming in a chocolate sea,

climbing cliffs at Mount St. Pea,

riding carpets through the stars,

or jumping rope on planet Mars!

But now I'm tired.
What about you?
Name four things you love to do.
Can you?